Hashtag What We Think

Compilers

Saurabh Madhavrao Jadhav
Ankumoni Das

BOOKSquirrel Publication

Hashtag What We Think

Book*Squirrel* Publication

Regd. Under MSME Act.

"Hashtag What We Think"

By: Saurabh Madhavrao Jadhav & Ankumoni Das

ISBN: 978-93-89557-61-9

Language English & Hindi

1st Edition

Formatting: Mr_Ash

Cover: Ronak Chavda

.

Disclaimer

This anthology is a fiction. The compilers have tried best to edit and curate the content of the co – authors and is made plagiarism free.

All write ups in this book are unique!

In case of any plagiarism detected neither the compiler, nor the publishers are responsible. Co – authors will be solely responsible for their own content.

Acknowledgement

4

The making of this Anthology would not have been possible without the co – authors and BOOKSquirrel team. I am thankful to Ashutosh sir, Rubal mam and Kshitij sir for making this project successful.

The hearty thanks to our parents, family, friends and off course all the co-authors for supporting us throughout this project. Love you all and #SpreadLove

Thank you to all authors

Part 01:
BOOKSquirrel Publication Anthology Department Head

Rubal Choudhary

This is Rubal Choudhary from Gurgaon, Haryana. She is 19-year-old and currently pursuing English Hons from Delhi University. She is a content writer and a co- author in 10+ Anthologies. She has Compiled two Anthology named- "Medley of words" and "Miracles from heaven". She is compiling 3rd Anthology on Mother's love.

Dear time, don't you get tired of running fast every day? Sometimes I compare you with the bullet train and sometimes with the speed of wind. For many you are good and for many you are bad, but the Irony is when I want you to speed up you always slow down! And this is the only thing which I cannot control in you!? Sometimes you move at the speed of blinking of my eyes, I know you pass by every day, every month, and every year and as we wish to grow more, you wish to grow less. We all plan big things, dream of a bigger success, carrier, house, traveling, marriage and many more and its totally because of you because you make me realize that I can do this in future. If I talk about past, I know many people blame you, out of no reason but they think that the condition was not as per what they thought. "Everything happens for a reason" even though many times we don't have reason but we have to understand and we cannot blame you and I really think how long you would walk along with me?? Humans are all controlled by you be it stopping, moving, pausing or whatever, you just handle them as per you. Sometimes you heal the wounds and maybe sometimes you don't but I wish each and every time you make me stronger. Just be as you are always!! Your well-wisher.

Part 02:
Compilers

Saurabh Madhavrao Jadhav

Published Author, Editor, Poet, Compiler. `Yashache Kshitij` is published by Rucha pub, Nagpur. `Prabodhan` handwritten book is published. Poems published in various anthologies like `Aksharangan`, `Troupe of Wishes`, `Aanchal`. Poems and articles published in various newspapers and magazines in Maharashtra. Known as Saurabh The SMJ.

Love

A simple combination of complication
Affection, Attraction, Dedication, Sacrifice, Love
A mixture and a cocktail of those feelings and emotions
If we like someone
We want them with us,
If we love someone
We want us with them.
It never occurs….
It happens….
Let fall in love
Let live the love
Let love the love
A love with expectations kills the love
No expectations destroys the love
The magic of love can't be shared until it's alike
Love is something that is love
Love is love.

Ankumoni Das

I am Ankumoni Das residing from a small town Goalpara, Assam. I am currently staying in Guwahati and pursuing my degree in Microbiology. Writing was never a passion but in due time it is something that soothes my mind and heart. I am a moody messed up soul who tries to penned down her thoughts not expressible in talks with friends and family.

Present scenario of a developing country

Equality 72 years passed, but do you think we are solely independent? The day , when the society will exempt patriarchy ; when transgender can live with outmost respect ; when religion , caste won't overrule love ; On that very moment we can say , Yes !! We are free; liberty has touched the feet of India. Parallel world's somewhere where women's' have conquered even the space and tall edgy peaks, brought crowns for country's pride. There are still places where women's' shield themselves in weighty veils, some are weighed in heaps of dowry, even unborn little feet are not allowed to step into this holy Earth. Where someone was ecstatic with even the defiled bread grab from the dustbin else ways some were still moaning about their continental cuisines! Child Labour: There are few who doesn't even take a glass of water on their own On the contrary There are those who work with their tiny hands just with the urge that they would not have to pass another night with empty stomach. Dowry Still there is some places in this country where our daughters are weighed in kilos of dowry. They burn each day in the fire of dowry searching for help but "What the society will say?". This mere line doesn't let their dear ones to help them out. Double Dealing One side where you stand for hours in the queue fasting the entire day, perform day and night vernation, sew beautiful garlands to please the goddesses and get her blessings. On the other side , while visiting the most sacred place you eve tease a lady , while standing on the queue you pinch someone , nowadays even the most holy place is not safe from molestation or harassment . The same world, where idols of women are worshipped and alive lasses are disrespected. Marital Rape When the most pure and sacred relationships are doomed in brutal crimes then there's only a option "Not to remain silent, coz this stillness might lead you towards the bed of eternal silence. Feminism The advocacy to provide liberty among the sexes. What's the use of providing this right when the other sexes have to face false accusations as we (the women) doesn't use this wisely. Indeed most of the parts of our country follow patriarchy, but that doesn't mean males are always the wrongdoer. Child trafficking Recruitment of a child for the purpose of slavery, forced labour and exploitation. Children are considered as forms of gods. But how can someone be so demonic that they steal this little wanderers to fulfil their dirty deeds. There are infertile couples who craves for conceiving babies rather there are parented ones who gets involved in this sorts of deeds only for a handful of bucks. Eventually, there are further more devastating problems surrounding our country, without the eradication of such blunders our country shall never be titled as developed.

Part 03:
Co – Authors

Dipannita Baishya

This is Dipannita Baishya presently residing in Guwahati, Assam. I basically hail from Tezpur.

When identify cards got replaced by visiting cards, black boards got replaced by desktop screens and PTA meetings got replaced by board meetings; time peeled off the mask of tranquillity to tension.

As she shuffled through the different dresses in her wardrobe to choose the right colour to make her monotonous life a bit more colourful. The white shirt and the grey skirt in the corner of the wardrobe reminded her of all the colourful memories that it scripted in her childhood and teenage years.

As the ring on her finger and a pinch of vermillion on her forehead scripted a new story in her life. The tattoo on her shoulder stated about something that she didn't wish to leave behind.

The locket in her necklace and the photograph in his wallet reminded them of one another every day; even though life flipped the page call "known strangers" for them.

Avani Singhal

An introvert who loves to write and a normal person who wants a big life than a long one. According to me only a writer is always faithful, at least to him/herself.

Virginity

What is virginity? Just having sex with someone... according to meaning-yes but being realistic for once, it's a word to describe a person's character in our Indian society. No matter if a person is kind -hearten, helpful and have a good attitude. If he/she is not virgin, then he/she is characterless. Especially if a girl is not virgin, she is characterless. I really want to know how does virginity defines character!! In my point of view, character can't be defined by virginity A bird called LOVE flies more above in sky than this small piece of shit called physical relationship. I think that is why People in love call it love making while people who are just hooking up call it sex. There is different type of people in this world everyone has a different point of view and has different situations too. Not everyone is strong, maybe the one who is not virgin is because she/he is raped. (Yes, u read it right. There are cases in which males are too molested but the ones who are at faults are those who did these cheap things for their pleasure.) Not everyone is smart; maybe he/she loved that person whole-heartedly and believes her/him blindfolded. Also, if these are not the situations it is that persons choice what he/she wants in life who r u to judge who r u to comment its his/her life and he/she knew better what is good or bad for them. Anyone has no right to comment or judge someone and interfere in their life. You can only decide if you want to be a part of that person's life and what part you want to be - memorable one or lesson one it's their decision and it needs to be respected. If a person is not virgin but loves you in present and wants to be with you and loyal and honest to you then how does virginity matter how does her past affects your future and the real question is why are u letting the past affecting present?? *Hone kyu de rahe ho?* Also , there is an amazing mentality in this society No matter if a boy is hooking up and having sex with some random chic for physical needs but

he needs a pure wife means yourself lose your virginity and that girl too she is losing her virginity may be with her own decision or in your love but partner - she needs to be clean and pure (and I don't know why these words are used - "clean and pure" what does that mean that the one 'non-virgin' is not pure how does not being a virgin makes someone impure?? Its mentality and bad things that they had done that makes someone impure) and then just say that "if u can sleep with me before marriage u can do it with someone else after marriage too" that's the permanent sentence when he don't want to marry her just want to hook her up are these guys for real , she is not double timing u , she loves u so she allowed u , she trusted u she is being loyal and yes may be no one has said this to u people ...but yeah girls can use the same sentence on u too and u know what the moment u show your true colours , these all same things reflects back on u and show how cheap ones mentality could be why this society always blames girl everyone has a different state of mind i know but only if u r virgin than u expect to be your future partner a virgin it's just a case but yes there are people in this world just 10% but yes they exist for whom virginity doesn't matter who love from heart to heart.. There are some people who are virgin but have partners who r not virgin this is called true love the one with a pure heart can have the courage to fight against all the odds and hold their partners hand to say "no matter who or what your past is , i m your present and that is all what i adore and now we will fight the past to live the present and to make happy memories for future" this is unconditional love that needs to be acknowledged and i salute this kind of love. So people "virginity can't define a person's character." change your outlook and respect every aspect of life as u are allowed to live your life your way everyone else is also allowed to live their life their way love people 'FROM heart TO heart' give respect and take respect. *"badnaam na kr ishq ko apni jism kikhusboun se ek yahi toh aangan hai jaha cheer haran nahi hota"* "love someone as what he/she is, not what u want him/her to be."

Jarnalisha Sutar

I'm Jarnalisha Sutar, an engineer and a cabin crew student also an immature writer. I write for the fact which makes me inspire. I write for myself and make one realize the fact in my mind.

You know what the main problem is with this society, indeed the thinking of the people. Indians do really think a lot. They think of every little thing which is no way connected to them. If you are an Indian you will get my view. Think of a situation cooking at home, whose figure do come in mind at first, definitely your mother or wife (I mean a women), but if I mention a cook, the figure is a men wearing a white cap white dress standing in front of food (stylish isn't it , but why is it a boy). Similarly, if I say sweeping the house the figure in mind is again a woman. But when I say a sweeper the figure is a man. Hundreds of examples are present to give. An engineer is always a man in figure and doctor is a girl. Actually, the fact is we have decided the person belong to one job. Like if I say I am a cabin crew everyone will think of a girl hostess but never a boy Stewart, why is it so. We know every job is equally influenced by both the gender of our society but you see the thinking of people have confined to a particular image. Actually, this image also indicates another fact that is if a job is done at home for free the person doing is a woman but when the same work is related to earning money the person is a boy. Why on this very big country of your the women is a non-earning part of our society even if every women works.

Akash Kedia

Akash Kedia is from Kolkata. He has completed his graduation and currently getting trained for his job. He loves sports like Cricket and Badminton. It has been his biggest dream to be an influencing writer. He basically writes Shayari, two liners, short stories, poems and quotes. He is one who loves to live life with simplicity. He accepts and deals with the challenges of life as his goal is to fulfil his every dream.

Reservation System

``The Biggest Reason for Country's Plight…. ``

I worked hard equally like others,
Never let anyone win by themselves,
My dreams remained as they were,
I became a hunt of reservation system.

People with 55% marks had smile on their face;
I was standing in a corner with 90% marks.
They got admission as they were part of reserved category,
But I could not get as I was out of reserved category.

Why don't they understand that it is an illusion
And country is suffering from this reservation system
Is there no value of those who want to get educated?
This is what I want to ask to the national political scholar

Every time they all just keep silence,
They have no answer to our questioning eyes,
Those who belongs to SC & ST will get the right,
What to say reservation system you are very nice.

No illusion this is a bitter truth that
Reservation has caused huge number of deaths.
Those who dreamt to be a CA doctor and engineer,
They went to lie for a long sleep on grave and pyre.

But the day when it will be too late,
They will say that we have now really realised that
Both the youth & nation are burning in the fire of reservation
And the future of whole India is completely destroyed.

Vaishno Singh

Vaishno Singh Student of class 10th. She is 15-year-old. Writing is her passion and she loves to explore the world with new colours of word

Hypocrisy does exist

First of all, the meaning of the word which has the main problem 'hypocrisy '? What does that mean, did it really exist? Then the answer will be yes, it's existed among the people living in the society of India. "HYPOCRISY" it is the main problem of our society because the people making it ill day by day. Have you ever noticed such kind of people as they pretend something and do something else opposite, that behaviour in which somebody pretend to have moral standards or opinion that he or she does not actually have? Why don't we realise only care   is not enough we have to take precautions because as we everyone knows precautionary is always better than care. Now days in social media people used to say if anyone not showing his or her patriotism in the media that means they don't care what is happening in their country. Is it true," NO" that doesn't mean they do not really care, yes of course they do but as they know it very well pretending like caring don't make the work easy? As the entire world knows how we Indians love our motherland so it is the time to show the seeds of Faith and wash away the dark sides of hypocrite. Let's being a role model for the future generation and take some important decision for the Welfare of our Indian society. Let's make our India not only prove and advance Technology also in positive thoughts having the carriage to do anything for the country because it's ours.

Prerna Chhetri

I love reading books, travelling; I'm a cosmetologist by profession. I've been writing for long time but never got serious. But 2019 I got to meet lots of writes that helped me understand how much I love writing. I have co-authored more than 5 books.

She was born

She was born from the dust,
Of a lustful street named Red-light.
Her mother was a beautifully crafted,
Grand gesture loved by many men.
None was her father figure;
They gave her no notice,
Her existence was a futile.

She was born from the wedlock,
Of a misguided act,
They say Love wasn't their profession,
Love making was her mother's name,
Her soul was lost in her teens,
She is a lifeless beautiful being;
Breathing in the hands of her lenders.

She was born from the sins,
The society utter,
While Fear never gave her way,
But her mother's unplanned womb,
Carried a life in a lifeless body,
"Beautiful mistake" she cried ,
Holding graces in her arms.

She was born with a future,
Written in hands of her lenders,
Our prized possession, like her mother.
Her numb body ached for first time.

Motherhood made her remember,
When they ripped her soul,
Turned into a goddess of flesh.

She was reborn with a future,
Written by her mother,
Rebelled against the order of society,
A first step in putting her girl,
For a freewill of knowledge.
She stands next to her proud,
Dodging the daggers of social abuse.

She was born to give life,
Like her mother, a little step,
Their future is fuelled by her,
With her knowledge and wisdom.
Taking with her together,
For a brighter tomorrow and hope.
No lenders to write their future again.

Pinky Ray

28

Hey there! I'm Pinky Ray, I'm a Bengali born Hyderabad. Writing is my passion and I love to express and satisfy myself by expressing my feelings!

Once there was a time, I considered myself an innocent one...but, after gazing you and you chasing my heart, I've been recklessly blind... The day you let me lay my heart in your soul the day you destroyed my silence the day you made me feel so mad and bad the day you molested me by your ignorance the day you broke me into pieces.... ~The journey with you was so utterly, beautifully brutal...   I may not be the perfect one, but thanks to you to making me realise that people these days are idols filled with pettiness and arrogance when are felt betrayed by the imitative beauty, which fades it's colours of joy...and breaks the idol into a deep understanding of their ocean of sorrow, filled with the waves full of sorry and realisation letters for them who once loved the idol them...!!!

One life, many decisions Many decisions, few choices Few choices, one aim. One aim which is mostly positioned by our saviours and those saviours are our decisions, which we make while seeing our parents sacrifice their time to build our aim and to make it secure... While this procedure we be a matured human!

Char Mahmud Khan

Myself Char Mahmud Khan from Goalpara, Assam and I am a law student

My Sleepless Nights

How could I close my eyes? When the eyes are blurry with the memories you left inside my heart. How could I sleep peacefully? When the heart is making noises loudly. How could it be possible for me? When I am deeply missing you. How could I leave loving you? When I had understood the meaning of love from you. How could I not be punished? When I had made a decision of being with you till and after my last breath. How could I enjoy every moment? When my pleasure and pain is with you... How could I believe my heart? When it lies and says that I hate you... How could I have a sweet dream? When my Sweaty and my dream is not you...

An Unconventional person

Fraternity neglected her. Fellowship never trusted her. Neither she had solidarity, nor did she can effort homogeneity. BUT, a simple word with doughty meaning she replied, "Enough" & decided to remain unconventional....

Nemika Sharma

Nemika Sharma holding Master's degree in English Literature and Creative Writing skills, born in a Small town called Padampur (Rajasthan) Since Childhood; she is enthusiastic & ambitious in making her career as Author. . As a young Author, she is full of emotions and passionate about real life learning throughout her experience. She believes that we can live our life to the fullest only if we understand true feelings deep inside without suppression.

अक्सर हर शाम

अक्सर हर शाम इक बच्चा मुझे देखता है आंखो मे कुछ सवाल है लबोपे
ना मुस्कानं है मैदान मे खड़ा ना जाने वो क्या सोचता है....
सोचा जाकर पुछ लू उसे ऐसा क्या है जो तुझे सताता है खेलने कुदने की
उम्रमे तु किन सवालोके बोझ ढोता है....
झिझकतेसे मुझे देखा कभी नज़र चुराता आहिस्ताआहिस्ता बोला शायद
कुछ दिलकी कहना चाहता है....
बेघर हू मै अकेलाभी भुखा ओर हूँ प्यासाभी अनपढ़ हूँ गरीब हूँ
क्यो रब हमे ऐसा बनाता है? जिसे देखो हुकुम जारी करता है नफरतकी
निगाहोसे मुझे निहारता है हर कोई दुत्कार जाता है बेमतलबकी फटकार
लगाता है....
क्या किया मैंने पाप है? क्यों कुछ भी नही पास है?
ऐसेही रहना होगा मुझे? क्या गरीब होना कोई श्राप है?
निशब्दसी खड़ी मै ना मेरे पास जवाब है उसका हर सवाल
और रोता चेहरा मुझे आज भी याद है....
गुजारिश है ये रब से तु सबका मददगार है
जिंदगी देदी है जिन्हे वो हर खुशी के हक़्दार है ....
आंसू नही देना किसीको सब तेरे कदरदान है
रहमत कर दे सबपर सुना है तु बड़ा मेहरबान है....

Ashish Seth

कहते हैं साहित्य समाजका आईना होता है तो मेरा निरंतर प्रयास रहता है कि मैं भावनाओंको शब्द दे सकू तथा मेरी क़लम वास्तविकताको प्रत्यक्षरूपसे कागज पर अंकित कर सके।

मुश्किल था

नीर था सबकी आंखों में, जब मैं दुनिया में आई थी,
और कहीं पालनेमेंही ना मार दी जाऊं, इस डरसे मैं घबराए थी,
अभिशाप नहीं परिवार पर मैं, यह समझाना मुश्किल था,
मेरे भी कुछ ख़्वाब है बाबा, यह बतलाना मुश्किल था।।

मैं जानती थी मेरे हिस्सेमें, चूल्हाचौका आएगा,
ज्यादा पढ़लिखकर मैं करुंगी क्या, इसलिए बस भैया पढ़ने जाएगा,
जंजीर बंधी नन्ही पंखोंसे, मेरा उड़पाना मुश्किल था,
और मेरे भी कुछ ख़्वाब है बाबा, यह बतलाना मुश्किल था।।

बचपनकी गलियां छोड़के पीछे, बडी़ हुई मैं यौवन आया,
पतझड़से मेरे जीवनमें, लगाके जैसे सावन आया,
मगर समाजके नरपशुओंसे, इज़्ज़त को बचाना मुश्किल था,
अरे! सांस तो आती थी हरपल, लेकिन जी पाना मुश्किल था,
आज़ाद घूम रहा था, वह जो सजाके क़ाबिल था,
और मेरी कोई ग़लती न थी, समाज को यह समझाना मुश्किल था।।

जीवन मुझे बताना था, पर किसी ने ना पूछी मर्जी मेरी,
जहां दहेज कम देना था, वहीं पर शादी करदी मेरी, श्वेतअश्व पर,
मेरे राजकुंवरका, अब सपनों में आना मुश्किल था,
और मेरे भी कुछ ख़्वाब है बाबा, यह बतलाना मुश्किल था।।

बाबुलके घर पर सुनती थी, कि बेटी तू तो पराई है,
और ससुरालमें सबने यही कहा, तू दूसरे घर से आई है,
क्युं अपनी होकर भी ग़ैर हूं, यह बात समझ ना पाई मैं,
आखिर वजूद क्या है मेरा, दिलको समझाना मुश्किल था।।

धर्मांतरण

नफ़रतके पिंजरेसे आजा़द, इंसानियतका परिंदा होता,
श्लोक,बर्स और आयत में, ग़र मज़हब कहीं जिंदाहोता।।

डरकी काली छांवमें, हर नारी रहती आजहै,
क्यों महफ़ूज़ नहीं हैवो, जो दो घरों की लाज है,
नफरत का पाठ पढ़ानेवाला, ग़र अपने किए पर शर्मिंदा होता,
तो यक़ीनन, नफ़रतके पिंजरेसे आजाद, इंसानियतका परिंदा होता।

चालाकीकी दुनियामें सब, मतलबके संबंध बनाए बैठे हैं,
रूह जिस चादरसे लिपटी है, उस में बेईमानीके पैबंद लगाए बैठे हैं,
ग़र इंसानको बस इंसान समझते, तो जहां ये बहुत उम्दाहोता, सचमे, तब
नफ़रतके पिंजरे से आजाद, इंसानियतका परिंदा होता।।

हथियारों भाषामें, अब होती सारी बातें हैं, और बारूदोंमें खा़क हो गई,
इंसानी ज़ज्बातें है, मैंभी बंदूक उठा लेता, ग़र गोलीसे कोई जिंदा होता,
नफरतके पिंजरेसे आज़द, इंसानियतका परिंदा होता, श्लोक, बर्स और
आयत में, ग़र मजहब कहीं जिंदा होता।।

Paakhee Sehgal

The writers name is Paakhee Sehgal. She is currently pursuing Bachelor's in Nutrition and Dietetics from Chandigarh University. She is a confident 19 years old girl who aspires to be a Star Dietician. She is born and brought up in Ambala city. She says that her love for writing and literature is inherited from her father. She is a Bibliophile (books lover).

Light to the Life

Sitting beside the window
Her eyes gleamed,
With felicity she whispered to sole...
Lights!!
What delect is in watching them making your world beautiful
The aroma in air is different these days, DIWALI
The setting of sun...
The pink orange clouds...
Shepherd's delight
The gleeful faces in the market crowd...
Selecting, Bargaining, Purchasing
But,
That day she saw some dreary, subfusc faces...
Sitting on one corner, they just imagined the world she lived!
Sighs...
Soul thoughts... Silence silences
Why not change the world,
Why not change the life,
Why not change the day,
Why not change the moment,
Let's bring some Lights to their life!

An Author

Itinerary sidereal day,
Life tune to its beat...
She stood in the corner observing...
Students mugging...
Birds chirping....
Musicians playing...
Grass dancing to the tunes...
Tangerine colour of the cloud's...
Dusk,
Shepherd's delight...
At night she sat down to the moon...
Wrote all what she observed...
That's what authors do...
Scribbling what they espy and envision!

RION

This is Rion kumar I'm 18 years old & I'm from Odisha but I have been studying in Visakhapatnam.just completed my diploma as a mechanical engineer and looking to do something new in life. Just want to travel as long as possible and explore new things on a road trip with my bike. These all writings are been written on someone memories and just want to dedicate to her. Thank you.

Everyone will say "move on" the person left you will never come back to you. But one will say never lose hope they will come to you they just need time. None other my inner soul to me.

The difference between two nights First one, after being into a relationship the night is full of happiness, Nervousness and Sleepless night full of excitement.   Second one, the person who whom you loved the most have been left you alone and thinking that she will be come back and a sleepless night full of pain.

1) Everyone will say that you deserve or get a better person than that who left you. But how can I explain that the person who left me is the best person I have met and understands more than anyone else.

2) We all living in the Era where we Men's cry silently more than Women. But still we carry a simple smile on face and nobody knows that we are crying.

3) You may think about hundreds of people throughout the day. But, when you go to bed and the person whom we think before us sleep is the most loved person in our life.

4) Still I have feelings for her in the corner of my heart & that corner has a big world for her.

Jayasree

I want to explore the society, wanted to learn how to face the society and want to aware the society

Dear moon,

When I will be down....
I need your accompany
When I will be low....
I need your accomany,
When I will be on heart break...
I need your accomany,
When I will be lonely....
i need your accomany,
Because no one is permanent expect you....
I know that you always love me...
Because though I leave you...
But you never leave me...
You always follow me.....

It has been so long but,

I was the same person....
Glimpses your profile picture while going to sleep.....
I was the same person...
Glimpses your last reply plenty time in a day...
I was the same person...
Waiting madly for your single reply....
I am the same person....
Always thinks about your career...
I am the same person....
But you changed...

Pankhi Sarma

This is Pankhi Sarma from Guwahati, Assam. An engineer cum writer is a self-published author and have co-authored many anthologies. She is a blogger, a content writer and by hobby she loves painting and clicking snaps!!!

Lost time

Dear Anonymous,
They haven't recovered from that change. Rather time moved on with the change ticking their life behind.

Poor deserted life was just there with no extravaganza, rom choms and the dim lights glowing over the darkness.
Neither love came by nor the hatred stopped by.
Jiya, Ankit, Rooh, Sahil, Punit were all lost and so their happiness. All at once a hurricane blew away their every single feeling. I was the one to witness all. I have foreseen them, their deeds their laughter and their luscious time.

How could have the time that gave the pleasure of immense moments an achievements, take away living not a penny behind. How deserted they felt was not comparable to mine.

I haven't been much of help. I regret to. Overseeing situations, panicking overnight, scary dreams is still what I'm going through. Though not comparable yes M also the sufferer in a way they did. Yes, that small prank, that small happiness cost their happiness leading and diving me into a depressed zone, no one reaching out again to me.

Could it have been the other way round or would I not have done that prank? Would they have been living now happily ever after music band with some loud show somewhere abroad?
Feeling sorrier admitting mistakes never has been my part since birth. Al I got was extra something and when I never got nay I snatch away all. Was that my fault? Creating tiffs, raising the flames high, shutting doors even after all shouted with their lungs

out. And I on the shore of ego and anger dived away from the love showered in time being..
I know all those times are bygones. Nonetheless, sufferings and ashes remained. With a guilty regret of not confessing at the right time but yeah an open letter to them after 4 years. May not the charges are taken off but can be diminished with this confession letter.

Yours, sweet bit
P....i

Richa Jain

Richa Jain, she was born in Kanpur, UP. And done all his education from here itself. She is HR by profession but as she loves to do lots of things she is an actress, blogger, YouTuber and of course a writer. Nothing is god gifts to her but she always made her way to get succeed. She is the part of few more anthologies like Orenda: The writers' league, the path you choose, The Blinding Dreams. After all she is good in her personal life too. Along with so many responsibilities she beautifully Manage her dreams.

खामियाँ

बेशक खामियाँ बहुत हों मुझमे,
पर प्यार तो तुम से करती हूँ।
तुम होगे सही हमेशा पर,
मैं भी कभी सही हो सकती हूँ।।

तुम कोहिनूर का हीरा हो तो,
मैं भी सच्चे मोती सी चमकती हूँ।
तुम एकलौते वारिस हो घर के,
तो मैं तुम्हारा वंश जन सकती हूँ।।

तुम अगर हो रूप नारायण,
तो मैं भी वन में रह सकती हूँ।
तुम हाथ तो बढाओ वादे का,
मैं पूरा करने की दम रखती हूँ।।

तुम हो सुबह की किरण से खिले खिले,
तो मैं सांझ सुहानी सी बहती हूँ।
पूरनमासी का चाँद हो गर तुम,
तो मैं रात ईद सी लगती हूँ।।

शराब पीना शान है तुम्हारी,
पर तुमको घर लाकर तुम्हारे जूते मैं ही बदलती हूँ।
भले तुम्हे पसंद हो कोठे की चमकती गुड़िया,
पर मैं पायल फिर भी तुम्हारे लिए छनकाती हूँ।।

फिर भी गर शौक है तुमको छोटे कपडों का,
तो मर्यादा मैं तुमको सिखलाती हूँ।
बेशक खामियाँ बहुत हों मुझमे,
पर प्यार तो तुम से करती हूँ।।

तुम जीना चाहते हो शान से,
मैं तुम्हे उड़ने का मतलब बतलाती हूँ।
तमाम उम्र गिनते रहना तुम मेरी खामियाँ,
आखिर में क्या खोया क्या पाया ये मैं गिनवाती हूँ।।

बेशक खामियाँ बहुत हों मुझमे,
पर प्यार तो तुम से करती हूँ।।

हिम्मत

हाँ हूँ बुलंद खड़ा हूँ मै,
चट्टान सा अड़ा हूँ मैं...
शाख छोड़ दे जो पत्ते जडों सा अटूट हूँ,
तिनक तिनक के गिर गए,
वो फूल सारे बिखर गए,
पर हूँ बुलंद खड़ा हूँ मैं,
चट्टान सा अड़ा हूँ मैं...

पतवार भी साथ नही,
राह भी आसान नही,
कश्ती डूबने को है,
चाबुक में अब धार नही,
पर हूँ बुलंद खड़ा हूँ मैं,
चट्टान सा अड़ा हूँ मैं...

वो धूल है थमी थमी,
वो डगर भी है रो पड़ी,
मंजिले थक सी गई,
आँधियाँ कुछ अब थम गई,
पर हूँ बुलंद खड़ा हूँ मैं,
चट्टान सा अड़ा हूँ मैं...

वो सूखते है खेत मेरे,
वो घर भी है सूना पड़ा,
यूँ झुलसती धूप में,
सांसो को भी रुकना पड़ा,
पर हूँ बुलंद खड़ा हूँ मैं,
चट्टान सा अड़ा हूँ मैं...

परिवार का अब साथ नही,
शहर बहुत दूर है,
यूँ अकेला इम्तिहानो में,
अकेला उम्मीदवार हूँ,
पर हूँ बुलंद खड़ा हूँ मैं,
चट्टान सा अड़ा हूँ मैं...

अभिमान अब खो चुका है,
किसी और गली सो चुका है,
मुश्किल नही थी राह कभी,
पर अब साथ सब का खो चुका हूँ,
पर हूँ बुलंद खड़ा हूँ मैं,
चट्टान सा अड़ा हूँ मैं...

Kirna Devi

51

Kirna Devi was born to a traditional Hindu family on January 6, 1992 in, Punjab (India). She did her M.A (English) from S.C.D Govt. College, Ludhiana. She has worked as an assistant professor Of English in Gobindgarh Public College Alour ,Khanna and also in Tara Vivek college Gajjanmajra. At Present She is working as a lecturer in Meritorious School, Ludhiana. Her Poem *'Kehne ko to Haseen hai Safar Mera' And 'Bharati Sabhyata ki Baat hi Nirali hai* ' has been published in e-magazine Of Delhi Poetry Slam.

The Shattered Heart

I remember those days
Of mesmerising evening,
The charismatic time we spend together,
Your innocent sinless smile
The long exotic conversations,
Our thrilled and captivated hearts
The winding paths we travelled together
And then the creeping insolence,
Neglect and tormenting desertion
Your incessant estrangement is like
Somebody was taking my soul out of me
I found myself adrift in the midst of the afflicted world
Your savage words kept haunting me day and night
The shattered soul wanted to know the abstruse reason
I the injured birds was left to fight the blizzard alone
The entombed emotions pricks like
The secret that left unspoken
I put fallacious masks on my face to show myself strong
But something kept flogging me inside
Your face appeared wherever i see
I was left with extinguished self that die with every beat...
Thought it has been a long time since we parted but
Still i wait for you
In the snowy evening to come and
Embrace the long buried fragmented me.

Dying Self

Aah !
Look,
How she is...
"Girl, you should be fair and tall", they say
They adore white as radiant, ravishing, resplendent,
Black is refused as imbecilic, horrendous, fearful nightmare,
You can't be loved, endorse, corroborated.
The unfathomed craving lay buried in the corner of morbid self,
They judge my symmetry
By the color of my sheathing,
Fails to enshrine the light of my soul
It lay rusted at bottom like the unrevealed treasure
Calling to be loved and adored,
I am a firefly
That fills the sky with its luminosity,
As the dawn approaches
It loses its luminosity and entity too.
I, the inauspicious broken idol
Put on fallacious mask
But some part of my self is dying inside.

Sagar Bhandare

Sagar Bhandare He is basically from a small town of Maharashtra 'SANGLI' which is known as NATYA PANDHARI (land of drama). He is an aspiring writer and willing to spread happiness through his thoughts, he is a keen observer and loves to pen his emotions, happiness, and fears. Sagar is someone who loves to read. He loves to stay positive and happy in every situation.

मुझे मत आवाज दो भीड में, मैं याहा खो जाना चाहता हूं।

मुझे मेरा अतीत मत पूछो, मैं नई पहचान बनाना चाहता हूं।

जिसे जाना है मुझे छोडके अभी चले जाओ,

मैं अपना वक्त खुद बदलना चाहता हूं।

यु तो बहोत अजमाया है किस्मतने मुझे,

अब मैं खुदको आजमाना चाहता हूं।

जितने भी दिन बाकी है साथ रहो दोस्तो,

अब मैं जिंदगी खुलके जिना चाहता हूं।

आदत हैं मुझे यु मायुस होने की, अब बस बेवजह हसना चाहता हूं।

उम्मीदली किरण तो हर कही है,

आंखे बंद करके आसमान छुना चाहता हूं।

मंजिल की फिकर अब किसे है,

अब तो मैं सफर में ही रेहना चाहता हूं।

फिर तुम्हारे इंतेज़ारमें

College के उस gate पे खड़े रहना चाहता हुँ,

फिरसे तुम्हारी आँखो में डुब जाना चाहता हुँ,

फिर से उसी मोड़ पे तुम्हारी आहट महसूस करना चाहता हुँ,

फिर तुम्हारी बातों में खों जाना चाहता हुँ,

कुछ ख़्वाब अधूरे ज़रूर रहें हैं हमारे..

तुम कहो तो फिरसे तुम्हारे प्यार में पागल हों जाना चाहता हुँ, माहोल ज़रूर बदला हैं..

पर तुम चाहो तो फिरसे तुम्हें अपनी आदत बनाना चाहता हुँ,

बहोत बार लफ़्ज़ जुबान पे आके ठहरे थे..

इस बार तुम आओ तो इज़हार-ए-इश्क़ करना चाहता हुँ,

दुरियाँ अब हम दोनो में हीं नहीं उम्मीदों में भी बढ़ गयीं हैं..

तुम मुस्कराओ तो दिल फिरसे तुम्हें देना चाहता हुँ,

आज भी यें दिल तुम्हारी याद में धड़कता हैं..

तुम क़रीब आओ तो फिर से तुम्हें एहसास दिलाना चाहता हुँ।

Kirtan Singh

56

Hey! I am Kirtan and I belong to the city of ghats - Varanasi. Poetry has really been a beautiful way of expression for me and it is going to be my favourite thing to do in leisure time. I hope you all like this piece here!

There's a reason

You had the courage to do it
And you gave it a try
For a reason unknown you failed in it
Tis' not a reason to hold back and cry.

The past has passed
And is past for a reason
Get up, move ahead and recast
Value time and don't cry for your depletion.

What happens in your lifetime?
Happens for reasons unknown
So let the cards unfold
Let your story be shown.

Feel lucky that it happened to you
It made you aware of the challenges misunderstood,
And for your mistakes gave a clue
After all, everything happens for our own good.

There's a reason for everything
There's a reason why this is happening to you
Look out for that invisible bling
To know why this life chose you.

Embrace the darkness

Every cloud has a silver lining
As after every nigh
Comes a beautiful morning.

But in the end,
Your perspective would amount,
It's about what you notice and what you discount:
A terrifying night that surrounds,
Or a beautiful morning that would soon be around.

So lose no hope after failure,
Take your time and upgrade by contrivance,
Let no hurry allure you,
For desired things demand patience.

When sometimes things go wrong a bit,
Rest if you must, but don't quit.
Think of the brightness it becomes,
And embrace your night that comes.

Shivam Sunil Bacchewar

Myself Shivam. I am doing B-Pharmacy. I like to write about this subject. I always want to share my words, feeling's with other.

जुनून

सीने में एक आग है, तू उसे अपने अंदर ही दबा रहा है,
उठा कर जमाने का बोज, तू खुद के सपनो को ही मार रहा है।
अरे, तु आग का समन्दर है, खुद में ही एक बवंडर है, तुझको कोई रोक
सके किसकी इतनी हिम्मत है? जानता हू घर का बडा है तु, सब की
उम्मीदो ने तुझे घेरा है, मगर जलाकर खुद का सपना,
औरो की उम्मीद पूरी करना क्या यही तेरा इंसाफ है।
अरे जिंदगी तेरी है, किसी के हाथ का खिलौना नही,
तु अपनी मर्जी का मालिक है, किसी और का गुलाम नही।
यूँ गौर नाकर दुनिया के बातो को,
तु तेरे सपनो को हकीकत में लाता जा,
इतना बडा आसमाँ तेरा सामने है,
तू सिर्फ पंख फेहरा और उड़ता जा।
तेरे लक्ष को तु ठानले, खुद के अंदर ही झाकले,
तुझसे कोई बड़ा नही इस बात को तु मानले।
जो तु चुन रहा है, समज ले वो आसान नही,
तकलीफो से भरा है, कोई खूबसूरत मकान नही।
दुनिया एक जंगल है, तु इस जंगल का शेर बन,
तकलीफो को जला सके ऐसी एक मशाल बन।

एक परिंदा

मोहब्बत में दो लोगों का मिलना जरूरी नही होता,
अगर इकरार ना हो, तो यंहा इंकार भी नही होता.!
हररोज बाते हो या ना हो, कुछ फर्क नही पड़ता,
प्यार सच्चा हो तो दूरियों का भी असर नही होता..!
मैं रहता तो उसके साथ ही हु, मगर कभी जताता नही,
मोहब्बत उस से बेइंत हा करता हु मगर कभी बताता नही.!
उसको हर रोज देखकर जिंदगी सुकून की गुजारता हु,
वो किसी और की ना हो जाये यही रब से दुवा मांगता हु.!
उसकी हर मनपसंद चीज मेरी मनपसंद हो जाती थी,
मुझे पसंद हो या ना हो येतो बाद की बात हुवा करती थी.!
उसका दिवाना मैं कुछ इस तरह हुवा करता था,
मेरे खयालो में वो हीर और मैं उसका रांजा हुवा करता था.!
उसको हर रोज देखकर जिंदगी सुकून से कट रही थी,
तभी एक दिन वो committed हो गयी ये खबर आने लगी थी.!
दिल ने अब सोचा ये चुप्पी तोड़नी ही होगी,
दिल में उसकी जगह क्या है उसे बतानि ही होगी.!
जब तक मैं उसे अपना दिल ये हाल बताता,
तब तक तो उसने कोई और हात थाम लिया था.!
मेरी कहानी का end तो start होने से पहीले ही हो चुका था,
इन सब चक्कर में सिर्फ उसके आशिक़ होने का
Tag सर पर लग चुका था.!
दोस्तो, एक तरफा प्यार का end कुछ ऐसे ही होता है,
वो हनारे कभी होते नही,
मगर ये दिल हमेशा के लिए उनका हो जाता है....!

Shiny Jaiswal

62

Shiny Jaiswal, a bibliophile going through books at top speed. Pursuing her graduation from MGIMT, Lucknow. She had co-authored in an anthology, "Thoughts that shaped you"

Betrayal

Deliberate, often calculated disregard of trust or faith. We all know its meaning but some of us know it better. It's like a throbbing pain slams into you and you reel back few steps losing your balance for a minute or an hour or a day or forever...... But eventually you gain it back and lead your life as if nothing happened but it'll never be same again. Never, there'll be this dull ache which will stop you from trusting anyone again, reminding you how it had hurt the first time and if you aren't a masochist, you will stop. And if you are, may God help you because there are many sadists in the world. Betrayal is not as dramatic as some people claim it to be. Your world doesn't come crashing down. It's more like cracks running all over your world, not breaking it but weakening it considerably. You try to cover them with beautiful wallpapers to make everything look fine. You ignore it because it hurts to acknowledge them. And the day everything finally breaks down due to those wretched cracks, you move on. Finally realizing there's nothing left to hold on to.

Why do we write?

You ask me, why do I write? It seems like a silly question to me. Why do you breathe? Why do you live? Why do you write? Do we ever have answers to these questions? You ask me, what do I write about? It seems sillier than the first one. Was there ever a boundary to restrict my writing to a single theme? Do you live your life around a single idea?   I write about from nothing to everything, from beginning to end, from never to forever. I never think while writing because that kind of ruins it for me. I let spontaneity take lead and I myself stand by amazed as words form and feelings take shape. At times it takes me by surprise that I write something so profound or so illogical. It could go both ways. It's not necessary that whatever I pen down is deep and hermetic, it could be downright stupid. A writer is never good or bad though your handwriting could be. To write anything you need to have felt it. You can't write something you've not even slightest indication about. It needs to be raw enough to touch the heart of your readers. Next time someone asks you why do you write tell them, life is difficult for gullible.

Atharv Avinash Pathak

65

Hey, this is Atharv Pathak from Pune. Connect with my on insta id (aths1803) . I speak the language of the tears that fall on your pillow each night.

Will rise again

Don't you dare, count me out
The first round has just begun
Can put me down, but can't keep me down
From my ashes, will rise again.

Afraid, ain't you, 'bout my comeback?
I know baby, can feel your pain
Can just put me down, but can't keep me down
From my ashes will rise again.

You got handed over everything from day one
But u know u ain't no perfection, and me ten on ten
That's why can just put me down,
But can't keep me down
From my ashes, will rise again

Ever saw a warrior, lay it all on the field?
Got nothing to lose or to gain
I am fearless and I am coming for you
From my ashes, will rise again

Ain't any need of favours
Always started with nothing at hand
But this time my sword will be mightier than my pen
U know it well,
Can just put me down but can't keep me down
From my ashes, will rise again

I'll be there to claim my throne back
Supremely and definitely, I will forever reign
Sad, that u can put me down but can't keep me down
From my ashes, will rise again

I ain't a saint baby; I am the demon that you fear
Come all guns blazing, but it would be in vain
Cause u can put me down, but can't keep me down
I am a Phoenix, from my ashes, will rise again.

Pratiksha Pandurang Sanap

Medico. Dream LBSNAA, reader, writer, civil aspirant.

From down to dusk

I saw her glance for a while
Which makes my heartbeat even she is far mile
Being lost in my own world is thus
From down to dusk it will be only us
You are sunlight, which makes the world live
And the gift from lord which was most expensive
In me, I am not alone, you are plus
From down to dusk it will be only us
You are my responsibility, you are my care
For you i can face any dare
In your absence, my heart becomes conscious
From down to dusk it will be only us
You will be my first priority
Till my last beat and even to eternity
For you, a place in my heart is obvious
From down to dusk it will be only us

दुरिया

हम दोनों है इतने दूर
कब आयेगा अपने चेहरेपे नूर
याद है तुझे वो अपनी गलिया
जहाँ कभी सपने थे सजाये
दूर हो कर भी हम है पास

सबकुछ लगता है अब इतना खास
याद आते है वो अपने साथ बीताये पल
होंगे क्या साथ हम कभी कल
कबतक देखेंगे अपनी अपनी राह
सब कहते अपने साथ को वाह
तू दूर है मुझसे मै तुझसे
सपना होता ये कभी काश
साथ हमारा केहलाता सबसे खास

Nilankana Medhi

Study: Pursuing bachelor's degree in English literature
Co-curricular: Graduate in Indian classical dance (Bharatanatyam), Performed nationally under ABSS, selected for the 7th Cultural Olympiad of performing arts, 2017 held in Spain. Resident of Assam. Hobby: reading

Odd days

I jotted down some lines on a few post-it notes years back. I stick them onto the walls of my room on days like today.

1. Wake up, do the chores, leave the house on time. On your way to class or workplace, check the plans. The date will strike; the memories may haunt but stay strong.

2. Smile back at people, talk, and hang out, despite the heavy numb feeling in your chest. Pay attention during the lectures or the meetings. Send the emails, take notes, prepare for the presentation. And when done, head back home.

3. On your way back, get the groceries. Don't stop by the wine-shop. Drinking won't help; it never did all these years.

4. After you reach home, freshen up, make a cup of coffee, read, work, chop the vegetables, make dinner, and eat. The routine.

5. Pick an outfit for the next day, set the alarm and strike another date off the calendar. The date will strike again. You may feel selfish for moving on. But don't bother yourself too much.

6. And in case, if your heart still aches, and tears are about to roll down your cheeks, read the letters they wrote to you, smell their clothes that you kept hidden on the third shelf; right corner of your almirah. And then go to sleep, for there when the lines between two worlds are thinner, may be they who left will come back to wave a hi. May be they will tell you that they are proud of you for staying strong, for smiling a little more, for being sober even in the madness of life. And that even if you have moved on, that's okay. So now go to sleep.

7. And don't forget to take down the post-it notes tomorrow. You have to learn to be strong without remainders, even on days like today.

It's been 4 years, I am still learning.

Kinjal Desai

73

Kinjal Desai is 21 years and lives in Gujarat with her mother. She is a Microbiologist embarking on literary career. She is sports enthusiastic and creation seeker. She writes to find the meaning of Life and Human love; this is about the wins and failures of her to understand Love. She thinks "Each appearance of you, explains the story you have traveled through".

MORE YOU!

The more you try to forget me,
The more you remember me.
The more you try to hate me,
The more you Love me.
The more you try to Get Away from me,
The more you get attracted to me.
The more you Get Angry to me,
The more you Fall for me.
The more you try to lose me,
The more you find me.
The more you try to be Negative for me,
The more you get Positive to me.
The more you try to give frowns to me,
The more you bring smiles to me.
I met you one summer,
For hours we sat and talked to each other.
The thought of your kind,
Ran through my mind.
The chapter of me was missing,
And you knew very well; my feeling.
The cry from the soul of you,
Out of truth; world view breaks into.
The incorporeal essence of us,
Traveled through each other's nerves.

Dhanyarashmi

75

I am Dhanyarashmi. I love writing poems. My passion towards writing is endless. My writing expresses love, positivity, and life thought.

Education is everything

The lands of Education sprouts the annual yielding
Today is the right day to throw ourselves
Into the lands of Knowledge
The seeds under the soil sprout out
Like a giant tree by consuming water and rain
In the lands of knowledge, dig yourself a arena
Sprout like a seed and visualize the light
Education is a path from darkness to light
Consume your mighty brain with knowledge
Education is everything
Let's Stand smart with innovation in Education Innovate yourself
like a bee sucking honey
Learn to the depth, and let your honey be sweet to the world
Under your Wings of knowledge, Shelter the others with
education
Being Smart needs some effort
Being literally smart needs tireless effort
Let's change the world through innovation in education

My all-time Visitor at my Door

Every month, there waits my visitor at my door
On certain days,
I am sure he will be standing on my floor
His arrival notified as if a burden at my back
My limbs grow powerless and painful
I drag myself to walk with pain
Something happens in my home
The paint of my wall becomes pale
I grow weaker and weaker when he nears
On the day of his arrival, he presents me
All the time, the same gifts of blood and pain
He keeps all those in my floor
And he closely watches me to endure
For more than five days
There is prominence of pain and stress in my room
My floors weep and scroll
I search for relaxation, peace and happiness
They were all the times at my door!
When this man steps in, they flee out!
Where have they gone?
They might be in some others door
The pain diminishes slowly
As he fades away in the darkness
My skin glows and my stress has burst into pieces
Every month, to show myself 'I am strong', he comes
I endure all, to extend my house for my generations' survival.

Divya Bharti

A nature lover who dreams to become a successful writer, Divya Bharti is one of those who believe in her signature line "If u can, u can..!" she is a student and pursuing her higher studies from Ranchi university. She has been a part of many anthologies as a co-author.

Fake feminism

We all are very familiar about the strongest weapon of a woman i.e. feminism. It simply defines the term equalism and justifies the sexism. But Now-a-days, new terminology has been added in our society and woman favoured it as brands i.e. fake feminism, which is a biggest and dangerous social issues trending in our peaceful country. This terminology contains two words fake and feminism. Those Girls misusing the power of feminism in the society just because of theirs ego gets hurt, which power has been created by the strengthen of society is the biggest problem kicked off in all over the state of the country. It is just about the wrong responses and steepest taken upon the male action which wasn't intentionally to hurt. It might be a mistake. I'm not a male lover or female haters' .I'm writing only against the wrong thought followed by wrong people. It is needed to be very aware about the fact before involving and supporting any matters. It might be Fraud..! There are three kinds of woman is surviving in our country and due to the third kind of woman, Youth are raising their voice against the feminism. Now, Questions arises here is If our society has term like Equalise as per our constitution, there from where this feminism has taken birth? And other questions should be asked that what is the reason behind .Still but why? Feminism is something that is totally different from what youth thinks. Today's youth need to be very aware about the conditions of the backward classes of women as well as forward too in 19th century. I agree that many laws and protections have been implemented in the favour of women but in spite of this, we women still face lots of problems that's why we necessarily or essentially need of the stuff like feminism. If protection, policy and laws crossing their number then why we should also be remembered and not forgetting that crimes has already been crossed their limits too. Feminism is simply "freedom". Everything has two aspects, positive and negative. Fake feminism is the negative part of it which undergoes the operation of equalise and sexism. It is basically Degrading the trust and power of feminism and lowering the Identity of women. It is not only harmful but dangerous also, it plays with the emotions, respect and feelings of someone man. Destroying the character of anyone by a fraud case is like a crime, exactly like the girl stalking for a brief duration by men is a crime in our country. Fake feminist's crime is dominating over the feminism trust. Don't show blind trust on female species. It can't be say that all men are good or bad, or even unable to say that all women are fake feminist just like the all men aren't rapist. In our country there's tendency of supporting and discussing any matters theirs own professional group members instead of the positive thoughts or right things. And that's a big mistake. We need to be understand the differentiate meaning of the word of feminism and fake feminism, which all depends upon the truth of words or the intentions. Don't get confused with the term feminism and feminize. Today, to identify a fake feminist is now a big and very risky task for the society..!

Men are men

They are like rain
Not all are same
Believe in him
Really they are men..!
We love the rain right?
Then,
We're trying to hate his presence,
Why we're denying his importance,
Why we'll not miss his absence?
Exactly they are men.
And men are men..!
Rain comes with clouds
As like men comes with hope,

Rain goes but brings the water
As like father go outside for a whole day

But brings the happiness for a family
Rain will save you from drought
As like brother save you from others right?
Rain is so sweet
As like the son of any mother,
Rain makes us alive
And men support us to live otherwise,
Sometimes, over rain turns into flood which are harmful too,
But still we love the rain,
Then, why not we love them?
And respect them?
They are human,
They have burden,
They are responsible,
They are special,
They have tears,
They have problems,
After all also,
His heart is full of emotions,
Yes,
70% homicide victims are men,
40% Domestic abuse victims are men,
85% homeless are men,
76% of suicides are men,
They are men,
Not all are same,
But
Men are men,
They are like rain..!

Rakshit Ghodkhande

82

Just a kind of person who's words can be better expressed through lyrics.

Because I

I am strong
Because I know
My weakness

I am beautiful
Because I am aware
Of my flaws

I am fearless
Because I have learned to
Recognize, Illusion from real

I am wise
Because I learn
From my mistakes

I am a lover
Because I have
Felt hate, and...

I can laugh
Because I have
Known sadness.

Sakshi Jain

A 17 year old, Girl Boss, trying of escapes the void of this confusing world. An interior designer and a Writer, always in search of a new frame to depict her creativity.

Escapism

A 22 year old girl, Milky White face as beautiful as a rising Sun. Rose pink glow where those red soft petals appeared with the perfectly shaped mountain and on the top of that those grey buttoned eyes were enough to catch anyone's heart in a snap. She was the happiest human being you will ever notice. Bestowed her life, improving the life of dogs all over the world. She worked day and night for every dog that came to her reach. She was doing this from past 3 years. But this was just window dressing, being happy every second was just her perfection of pretending. In pretending her emotions, she was as perfect as she was in her work. The lie came in sight when she met this boy and felt in love with him, again. When they met, the boy noticed scars and bruises on her wrist and ankles, and eventually on her whole body. There were scars in her body more than stars in the sky. One day, out of curiosity, the boy asked her about her scars. She has never told her truth to anyone but neither could she resist herself from speaking the truth to him. She said in a hush voice," these scars are my punishment. These are all done by me to myself, out of anger, guilt and regret." With teary eyes, she further continued saying "That was a murder. I killed him. Dark night, heavy rainfall, I was driving and we were reaching home. On reaching, he jumped out of the car and then I was parking the car. But suddenly I heard a scream and noticed that something has hit my car. It was him. He was lying dead in front of me. I was numb. I killed him." Her only love, her companion was dead. Yes, he was none other than her companion, her dog, Bob. And that scars were her punishment by herself for killing Bob. Though it was an accident but she concluded herself as a murderer. After that day she bestowed and surrendered her life to dogs so that she could escape her guilt of that night, the Murder.

Prathamesh Shinde

87

Prathamesh D Shinde (Buddy)... Moody Author.... Medicohelic... Civil aspirant ... Work as social worker..... #INSTAGOOD.

शेहर की उस ज़ानिब अब माहौल कैसा है?
पेहले सा है या कुछ बदला भी है?
वो जो सड़क बनने वाली थी बन गई या अभी बाकी है?
ये हमने जो घर बदल लिए है आपस मैं,
ये घर अभीभी अपना नही लगता.
उस घर की बहौत याद आती हैं.
उस तरफ आने का मन तो करता हैं
बहौत मगर ये मुझे जाने नही देंगे.
रात को तो ज़्यादा परेशानी होती हैं.
नींद भी आती नही, अब ये शेहर पता नही क्यों अपना नही लगता. और
ऐसे में तुम भी नही रहते अब यहा ज़्यादा तो डर भी लगता हैं. अकेले
रहने की आदत नही हैं ना.

Nishant S Pal

89

Myself master Nishant S Pal from thane, Mumbai pursuing medical education in "AYURVEDA". Achieved silver medal in "CAMLIN" arts festival 2016-17."INVEST IN YOURSELF. IT PAYS THE BEST "interest". I adore being who i have born to.

Now is the moment...

Life is auspicious that happened to you..!!
Retrieve the essence of amusement my "TROOP".
Explore life by being a "LIFE"..!!
This is the moment to authentically "FANTASIZE".
No tomorrow, no future you retain..!!
This is the only moment to open up the life-like "CHAMPAGNE".
So, why to wait for the moment to come..!!
Now is the very moment to "ASPIRE" the fun.
Ups and downs are part of "QUEST"..!!
Be fearless to give your best.
Clinch opportunity to "THRIVE" from within..!!
Indiscriminate choices can make you keen.
Last and whole the universe is here..!!
Put the "MEDAL ON THE PEDAL" to sheer.
This is the short verse for my dear "ALLIES"..!!   Accomplish life
by being a "LIFE"!!!!!

Dipak Prakash Kumbhar

91

I am Dipak Prakash Kumbhar. Student of Ayurveda and studying at Late Kedari Redekar Ayurvedic College Kolhapur. "I don't know how I write, but I know how well I express it". Writing is not my business, it is passion for me.

Life

What is life? When I asked this question to myself then I was just blank for few seconds and my whole body was shivering. I don't know the exact reason for this but I entered in to the depth of my mind and just thinking about life. Lastly I conclude that life is nothing but experiences and every experience creates new way to understand the life. I think that in this world no body is perfect; if anybody becomes perfect then it is perfect. If you have lots of experiences then memories can be created automatically and every memory will be full source of joy. Life isn't simple what we are considering, but it can be simple if we think simple. Life is not just four letter world; it is identity for every person. If you find the exact meaning of life then you will be at the place of great persons like Dr. Abdul Kalam sir, Swami Vivekanand and like many other people. They dedicated their lives for their country and for the every people present in it. Change is the law of nature and every change at every movement creates new things in our life, that things may include joy, sorrow, fear, thriller etc. Which try to say that life is very beautiful and enjoy it at every moment as per your own way doesn't follow others because everybody is unique. Every person has survived in a different environmental condition so that environment helps to shape their lives and make them achieve their goals. There is great connection in between life and nature if you once know the connection between them then nature will keep you in that position where nobody can reach. So, enjoy your life with full of satisfaction, don't get depressed and be faithful with yourself.

Sanket Dattatray Shelar

This is master Sanket Dattatray Shelar from Belwandi Bk. A. Nagar Maharashtra achieved first prize in speech competition organised by Maharashtra Government in 2010-11.Attended 3-4 poet conference, also got prizes in them. I admire to become a poet and an artist

मै जरूर चाहुंगा...!!

मैं नही चाहता,
कि तु मुझसे यु हर दिन फोन पर २-३ घंटे बात करे,
तु हर रोज मुझे मिस यु, लव्ह यु कहे,
लेकिन मैं ये जरूर चाहुंगा कि सुबह सुबह आनेवाला तेरा सिर्फ गुड
मॉर्निंग का मेसेज मुझे दिन भर कि उर्जा देकर चला जाऐ।

मैं नहीं चाहता,
कि तु मेरे साथ डेटिंग पर चले, मेरे साथ सेल्फी खिचाऐ,
गोल-गप्पे खाऐ लेकिन मैं ये जरूर चाहुंगा कि
में जब भी तुझे देखुँगा ना तो चेहरे पे वो हल्की सी मुस्कान और ओठों
पर वो प्यारी सी हसी आऐ

मैं नहीं चाहता
कि तेरी हर झपकती पलकों के साथ तु मुझे याद करे, तेरी हर साँस में तु
सिर्फ मेरा ही नाम लिखे लेकिन मैं ये जरूर चाहुंगा की, जब भी में तेरे
पास आऊंगा ना तो तेरी तेज हुई दिल कि धड़कन और बडी हुइ सासों
की रफ़्तार हमारे बीच के प्यार का इजहार करे

मैं नहीं चाहता,
की मेरे हर मेसेज का तु जल्दी से मुझे रिप्लाई दे, मेरे हर पसंद-नापसंद
का तु खयाल रखें, मेरे जन्मदिन पर पहला विश तेरा हो लेकिन मैं ये
जरूर चाहुंगा, कि एक दिन में तेरा हात-हातों में थाम लु और एक बार
सिर्फ एक बार तुम्हारे कानों में हल्के से कहु कि, कितनी खास हो तुम
मेरे लिए।

मैं नहीं चाहता कि,
तु याद रखे वो हर लम्हे, वो हर पल जो हमनें साथ गुजारे है,
वो हर ख्वाब, वो हर सपने , जो मैंने तेरी आँखों से देखे थे।

लेकिन मैं ये जरूर याद दिलाना चाहुंगा
वो दिन जब हम दोनों किसी समंदर पे गए थे,
और वहा पर तुमने रेत पर एक प्यारा सा दिल बनाकर उस में हम दोनों
का नाम लिखा था और समंदर कि लहरों की वजह से वो मिटसा जाता
था, और मेने कहा था ये लहरें क्या पुरा समंदर भी हम दोनो अलग नहीं
कर सकता।

Khushi Pathak

I'm a budding writer and I love writing poems which are related to real life incidences. Writing poems is my favourite thing to run away from the reality.

Alone

All alone in the house
Which was full of people chattering
Her mind was heavy to carry
Which people didn't realise were mattering
She had her heart full of vain
Which she kept from everyone
Even though she tried to express
But her last hope even had sunk
She wanted to live with peace
A life when nobody doubted her
The only thing she wanted was trust
Even when being truthful was a blur
She stopped sharing things
And hid her emotions inside
Even though it just killed her life was a hard ride
Nobody would've interpreted misinterpretation
The way she did everyday
A fighter rose under her skin
As she fought battles everyday
She wanted to stop the life she lived
And wanted to run far away
But the god isn't that grateful
And in the same house he made her stay
She had gone through a lot
Which she didn't even deserve
After all what kind of life is it
When it doesn't get on your nerve

What is it being a woman

What is it being a woman
What is it being a woman
Even when you don't get much respect,
What is it being a woman
Even when you are kept in suspect;
What is it being a woman
Even when you don't get to dress up the way you want to,
What is it being a woman
Even when you can't get a day off or two;
What is it being a woman
Even when you tolerate other's anger,
What is it being a woman
Even when you get beaten by hanger;
What is it being a woman
Even when you have loads of responsibilities,
What is it being a woman
Even when you can't show your abilities;
What is it being a woman
Even when you need other's permission,
What is it being a woman
Even when you manage things in the worst condition;
What is it being a woman
Even when you can't follow your dreams,
What is it being a woman
Even when you suffer through extremes;
What is it being a woman
Even when you can't stand for yourself,
What is it being a woman
Even when you can't live a life for thyself....

Vyomika Pandey

I am a girl from, the spiritual capital of India also known as Kashi. Writing gets me going, and I always find writings beautiful and pristine.

The letter I wrote

I've written you,
A bunch of letters
Describing my emotions
And how my heart, in a rhythmic fashion, flutters.

I've known you for a while now
Like, I've known love, an old mate
It's pretty beautiful, and so are you
And I've fallen for both of you
In magical ways.

I've known the tragic ending of Romeo and Juliet
Like I've known love, a disastrous fate
And I've fallen for Shakespeare's words
Like I've fallen for you
But it's the danger for which I await.

I've written you,
A bunch of letters
Mistaining and misspelling the words
I wanted to say.

The first letter I wrote
Described my love for silence,
Mystical silence.

The second letter,
Described my love for
Food, 'Ruhe' and Rose.

The third one included
The lyrics of my favourite song
Poems by Blake and Neruda
And lines from my favourite prose.

The next five letters, described
Spring, flowers and songs
Gazals and shayaris by Faiz, Mirza, Iqbal
And a whole letter containing lines by Gulzar-

'koi khaamosh zakhm lagti hai
Zindagi ek nazm lagti hai'

Remember?

The last letter I wrote
Titled- 'A letter of love, from love'
Is still with me
It talks about your pristine soul,
Serene Eyes
Talks about my incidents with love
And contains a secret which will always remain on hold.

I've known you for a while now
Like I've known love, an old mate
It's pretty beautiful
And so are you
And I've fallen, for both of you
In magical ways.

Kshitij Singh

I'm a teenager. I use writing as a medium to escape from reality. I write for my own pleasure.

The Only wish

Cross legged,
With hands under my head,
Under the starry sky I laid,
Looked at the stars,
Blinking,
With them blinking back
I saw one falling from a far,
Made me wish only one thing.

Next day,
I saw your eyes,
Filled with stars,
In a dark purple sky,
Oh it got a grip on me,
The way you smiled,
As the your rays hit me,
Oh how I shied,
And blushed.

The radiant smile,
That you possess,
A magnet which my heart,
Made of titanium, Couldn't resist
Became my reason to live.

The pen, the paper

I thought I'd stay away from this pen,
I thought I'd stay away from this paper,
But once again
It all was in vain,
How he plays with us
This game of life
I thought I'd stay away from this paper,
I thought I'd stay away from this pen.

Everything I once worked for,
Shattering like a glass...
Deformed like sand,
Falling through my fingers,
Can't hold it...
It rushes down from my hands...
My fingers, they shiver
I thought I'd stay away from this pen
I thought I'd stay away from this paper.

I feel so empty,
Like there's nothing else left to do.
So I sit and think about my life,
Which brings me back to the Oblivion,
Seems like I'm losing this wager,
Everything seems like,
Pushing me back to the pen and the paper

Anshika Anand Singh

Hey! This is Anshika Anand Singh. I am a resident of holy city of Varanasi. I write poetry to escape reality. At times, I fit into lyrics more than I fit into my life. Besides writing, I love to paint and travel.

Things I found in the basement

I found an old key
In the basement today
It looked Red and Brown
With all the Time painted on it.
It left a weird smell on my hands.
Smell of the old hands
Of the power to unlock.
I heard someone
Knock the door
I felt the touch
Of someone who was
Waiting to come out for years.
I felt someone walk
Out of the room leaving behind
A bundle of thread he
Used to knit life together
I held the key like it
Had a story to tell.
It reminds me of how
Few things unanswered
Are still beautiful.
How old things carry Infinite yesterdays.
How every tomorrow is going to be history?
I found an old key in the basement...
I carry it everywhere I go now.

People

Who are they?
If not metaphors
Wandering in the hallways
And alleys.
Are they made up of
Laughter they fake
And the lies that they make?
Or the eyes drown in stardust
But heart covered with past-rust?
Aren't we all on this path?
To the death
Inhaling, exhaling
Breaking, collecting
The pieces that either
We get broken in
Or the ones that we lost,
And then, one fine day,
When it becomes too hard
To carry on,
We all stop
Right there.
And turn into a single line
On a monitor.
And get mixed with the sand of graves.
Where we all are one,
Without any differences.

Jyotirmaya Pani

Hello! My name is Jyotirmaya and I enjoy moonlight strolls on the beach, red roses by the armful and participation dances... Just kidding I am not a fan of any of those things. Interestingly any combination of 26 alphabets won't explain me... More seriously my friends would rather explain me better... a good listener... a tech enthusiast and a good bad boy... Pursuing my graduation in Siksha o Anusandhan University!!

"Down the memory lane"

There was time when we used to hate certain things in our life even if we knew we can't change it...now when we knew we can change certain things we are loving it unconditionally... It was the time of summer, in one hot afternoon while relaxing sudden call came from friends that they were planning to go for Ladakh trip next month. As it was so hot in our locality everyone including me was quite happy that we were going to a new and cold place for enjoying our vacations...while everyone was thinking about the budget I was thinking how to explore that place... Everything was well prepared and hangouts with friends were one of the splendid movements anyone can have in their life irrespective of everything therefore everyone was quite excited... But all of a sudden a sad demise of one of our beloved friends parents bought everything in its knee and the entire plan was in vein... Unfortunately we couldn't fulfil the plan, but it does created and kept a separate place in my heart to cherish it all along.. Whenever I will have an opportunity to spend days with friends and explore the world I will surely be a part of it!!

Dibya Probin Dihingiya

Hello, Myself Dibya Probin Dihingia, presently pursuing my second year MBBS @ TMCH, ASSAM. Sometimes you have to make yourself flow with the lyrics of your mind and that's what I do. I am not a regular writer but when heart and mind comes in a bonding words flows out automatically... A page from my old friend (my diary) who understands me and my situation. Hope you like the content!

Heartbeat

Come and listen to my heartbeat
It still beats for you
Come near me don't go apart
I still wish to have you
Come and talk to me
I wanna hear your voice
Come and love me
I don't wanna make a second choice
Come and heal my wounds
It hurts a lot
Come and hold my hand
I miss you the most
Come and console me
I need your care
Come and convince me
I am in darkness and despair
Come and slap me
I am broken into pieces
Come and hug me
I feel lonely in your absence
Come and be in my dream
I will smile
Come and be my princess charm
I will walk with you miles
Come and stand with me
In my hardest time

Come and support me
I will be alright and fine
Come and hypnotize me
I'll do what you say
Come and lift me
Or else I'll die every day!

Mihika

Hey! This is Mihika. I have been a debater, an anchor and have participated in many speech-oriented programmes and look forward to many more. I find peace in writing as I feel that pages are the best listeners.

बात करी आज एक गरीब से,
हाथ धुले हुए थे नसीब से।

ना थी रोटी, ना मकान था,
फिर भी चेहरा हसीन था।

जो ना था उसका दुख ना मनाया,
जो था उसकी ख़ुशी में समाया।

पूछा मैंने सुनो ए जनाब,
क्या देखते नहीं पैसों के ख़्वाब?

बोला मुझसे क्या हैं पैसों में?
होगा क्या गर बन जाऊ अमीर मैं?

बड़ी गाड़ियों में घूमते है,
अंग्रेज़ी भी बोलते हैं।

पर आखिरकार इंसान ही इंसान को,
हिंदू-मुस्लिम में तोलते हैं।

प्यासे से पानी से पहले,
जात उसकी पूछते है।

चारों धर्मों का नाम जोड़कर,
इज़्ज़त औरत की रौंदते है।

फ़ायदा क्या है इस अमीरी का,
जो प्यार करना ही भुला दे।

ऊँच नीच में फ़र्क बता दे,

जन्म से पहले ही धर्म का थप्पा लगा दे।

इससे अच्छे तो हम है बिटिया,
सबको देखते बराबर नज़रिया।

इंसानियत एकलौता धर्म है,
फ़र्क बहुत है, साथ मगर है।

शाँत खड़े सुना सब कुछ,
मानो फ़कीर सुना रहा हो।

चंद पलों में वो मूझे,
जीवन की कहानी सुना रहा हो।

जीवन पाठ पढ़ा रहा हो!

धूप में खड़े थे कुछ वक़्त,
तब छाव की कीमत जानी है।
दर्द का जब एहसास हुआ,
बेदर्दी की ऐश तब पहचानी है।

चाहे रास्ता हो बेहद लंबा,
मंज़िल भी तो आएगी मगर।
खूबसूरती पर ऐतबार भी तभी होगा,
जब लग जाएगी उसे भी नज़र।

नींद भी है आराम के लिए,
पर सुकून तो कितना कम है।
खुशियों की एहमियत वही जानता है,
जिसके हिस्से में थोड़ा ग़म है।

जुनून की बेहोशी में ही,
कुछ कर दिखाने का होश है।
अनकहे थोड़े राज़ है,
तभी बातें बहुत मदहोश है।

दुनिया का है यही रिवाज़,
अच्छा-बुरा है दोनों एक साथ।
चलो बदल के देखे सोचने का अंदाज़,

हुए है बर्बाद, तभी तो है बिंदास!

Ankur Srivastava

Ankur Srivastava (अंकुरश्री), twenty six years young philosophical writer and poet, born in AnandNagar, in district Maharajganj of Uttar Pradesh. He graduated in education from Digvijay Nath P.G. College, DDUGU, Gorakhpur. He is a renowned teacher with an experience of about 10 years in teaching in different schools of the town. He got published his two poems in the anthology "Whishpers at Midnight" compiled by Abhijit Kumar Parvin. In his notion, "Writers are those whose weapon is Pen."

जानना

प्रतीत होता है
कि कभी कभी
ना जानना सबकुछ,
बना देता है
आपकी ज़िंदगी को
थोड़ा आसान।

अगर लगता है कभी
जानते हैं सबकुछ,
कुछ पल के लिए,
आ ही जाता है,
मन में भयभीत
मिथ्या अभिमान।

ना जानना उसे,
जिसे सब जानते हैं
और जानना उसे हैं
जिसे कोई नहीं जानता,
समत्व में
रखता है मान।

धानी रंग सी खिल जाओ

दो पल के लिए ही सही,
तुम मुझमे समा जाओ;
ऐसा कि मैं तुम हो जाऊं
और तुम मैं हो जाओ।
अलग ना कर सके कोई,
घुल मुझमे ऐसा जाओ;
डुबूँ जो तुझमे मैं,
तुम धानी रंग सी खिल जाओ।